Ashlyn Grows... Cherry Tomatoes

by

Gene Powell

Illustrations by
Mike Motz

For my wife, Jamie,
whose love and support
made this book possible.

Ashlyn Grows... Cherry Tomatoes

Ashlyn is having dinner with her mom, dad, and her brother, Jackson. "Mommy, what are those red things on our plates?" asks Ashlyn.

"They are cherry tomatoes. They taste good and are good for you, too," Mom says.

"Where do they come from?" asks Ashlyn.

"They grow on a plant," Dad says.

"Can I grow cherry tomatoes?" Ashlyn asks.

"I'm sure you can," says Mom. "Let's call Grandpa after dinner and see if he will help you."

Grandpa goes over to Ashlyn's house to help her with her project. "Buckle up!" says Grandpa as he helps her get ready to go.

"Where are we going, Grandpa?" asks Ashlyn.

"We are going to drive over to the Garden Center to see Mr. Wilson," he answers. "He will help us with all we need to grow cherry tomatoes."

"Hi, Mr. Wilson," says Grandpa. "This is Ashlyn, and she would like to grow cherry tomatoes. However, her mom and dad have very little room for a garden. Would you help us?"

"Hello, Ashlyn," says Mr. Wilson. "I would be pleased to help you. First, we will get a container to put the plant in so you can put it anywhere in your yard your mom and dad would like. Second, we'll get some potting soil. Then we will pick out the best cherry tomato sprout for you and a tomato stake to hold the plant up."

They all walk over to a big selection of pots. Ashlyn runs to one in a color she likes. "May I have this one?" she asks in an excited voice.

"Certainly!" Grandpa says.

Mr. Wilson adds, "This is a perfect container for your plant."

They then grab a bag of potting soil and a tomato stake. "Do we need anything else?" asks Grandpa.

"Oh yes," says Ashlyn. "We need to pick out the most beautiful cherry tomato plant here!"

And she does!

Grandpa pays Mr. Wilson for the materials.

"Thank you, Mr. Wilson, for helping me with my project," Ashlyn says.

"You are quite welcome," he responds as Grandpa loads the car. Grandpa then drives Ashlyn home.

"I can't wait to show Mom and Dad and Jackson what we bought today," she says.

"Tomato plants like very warm weather," says Grandpa. "And since it is past the 'last freeze date' in our part of the country, we are going to go ahead and plant the cherry tomato plant now."

Ashlyn shouts, "Hooray! Hooray!"

Grandpa explains, "We first need to check for a weep hole at the bottom of the pot. If it doesn't have a weep hole to let excess water drain, we will have to make one with a drill. Next we need to put a big, flat rock at the bottom of the pot and cover the weep hole. This keeps the potting soil from falling through the hole but lets the water drain."

Ashlyn asks, "Can I put the potting soil into the pot and pat it down?"

Grandpa answers, "Yes, you may. And once you are done, dig a hole in the soil so we can place the roots of the tomato plant there."

Ashlyn says, "This is fun," as the two of them gently tamp the soil around the plant to secure it in the pot.

Grandpa puts the tomato stake in the pot and then Ashlyn asks, "Are we done?"

"We are done with one big exception," says Grandpa, "watering the plant!"

"I'll do it!" she says as she gets her watering can, fills it with water, and waters the cherry tomato plant. "I will check the cherry tomato plant every day to make sure the plant has enough water," Ashlyn promises.

Every day Ashlyn tells her parents, "I need to go out and check my cherry tomato plant." And every day she does, just as she promised Grandpa. "Wow!" she says to her parents. "Every day the plant looks bigger. The plant started off much smaller than me, now it is much bigger than me!"

And as Ashlyn looks closely at the plant, she notices little green tomatoes. "Wow!" she says. "I will soon have some cherry tomatoes to eat."

"I like Independence Day," says Ashlyn. "I get to hear stories about the brave founders of our country, and I get to stay up late and watch the fireworks."

Mom says, "We invited your aunts and uncles, your nieces and nephews, your grandparents, and some friends over to celebrate the 4th of July with the family. Dad will cook out hot dogs and hamburgers and corn on the cob, I will cook the baked beans, and we will also have potato chips, watermelon, and homemade ice cream that Grandma makes."

Ashlyn answers, "Hooray! Hooray! And I will help!"

But this Independence Day is even more special. She has a big surprise to show Grandpa. "Grandpa! Grandpa!" Ashlyn yells with excitement as he walks around the corner. "I have something to show you."

Grandpa smiles and asks Ashlyn, "What is it?"

She takes him by the hand and says, "Come with me."

They walk hand in hand to the patio and to the cherry tomato plant, and lo and behold . . .

. . . there are red tomatoes on the plant!

Ashlyn jumps up and down with excitement as Grandpa looks closely at her treasure.

"What a wonderful surprise!" he says. "Are you going to pick one and eat it?"

Before Ashlyn answers him, she grabs a tomato and eats it. "Mmm," she says. "That is so good!"

She picks the rest of the red tomatoes and takes them to Mom and Dad.

"What a surprise!" Dad says. "We will put these on the table and shares them with our guests."

Ashlyn says, "Good! I want to share my cherry tomatoes with everyone!"

All through the summer and early fall, Ashlyn waters the tomato plant and picks tomatoes. "Here, Mom. Here, Dad," she says as she hands a basket of freshly picked fruit to share with her parents, her brother, Jackson, and of course, her Grandma and Grandpa. Make no mistake, Ashlyn ate a lot of the tomatoes, most of them right off the plant!

Grandpa tells Ashlyn, "The tomato plant will start getting tired in the fall, and when the first frost arrives, it will no longer grow tomatoes. This is the time we pull the plant out of the pot and store the pot in the garage for the winter." That day arrives and Grandpa helps Ashlyn take care of the work they need to do to close out the growing season.

Although it is not the happiest day for Ashlyn, she knows the growing season is over. "I cannot wait until we can grow more tomatoes," she says to Grandpa. "Will you help me again?"

He answers, "I certainly will."

"I love you," says Ashlyn to Grandpa.

"I love you, too," he says to her.

Ashlyn takes Grandpa's hand. They walk down the patio hand in hand, turn the corner and go into the house. Next year is not very far away.

Made in the USA
Charleston, SC
27 June 2015